J
3-4th
K ROLL

The Hit and Run Gang 2
GANG
PLAYING FAVORITES

STEVEN KROLL grew up in New York City, where he was a pretty good first baseman and #3 hitter on baseball teams in Riverside Park. He graduated from Harvard University, spent almost seven years as an editor in book publishing, and then became a full-time writer. He is the author of more than fifty books for young people. He and his wife Abigail live in New York City and root for the Mets.

The Hit and Run GANG 2
PLAYING FAVORITES

STEVEN KROLL

Illustrated by Meredith Johnson

AN AVON CAMELOT BOOK

For Ellen Krieger

THE HIT AND RUN GANG #2: PLAYING FAVORITES is an original publication of Avon Books. This work has never before appeared in book form.

AVON BOOKS
A division of
The Hearst Corporation
1350 Avenue of the Americas
New York, New York 10019

Copyright © 1992 by Steven Kroll
Illustrations copyright © 1992 by Avon Books
Published by arrangement with the author
Library of Congress Catalog Card Number: 91-93024
ISBN: 0-380-76409-1
RL: 2.8

First Avon Camelot Printing: March 1992

CAMELOT TRADEMARK REG. U.S. PAT. OFF. AND IN OTHER COUNTRIES, MARCA REGISTRADA, HECHO EN U.S.A.

Printed in the U.S.A.

OPM 10 9 8 7 6 5 4 3 2

Contents

1. A Gust of Wind

Top of the sixth. Runners on first and second with two out. The Rah Rah Rockets trying to hold a 3–2 lead over the Bradford Tornadoes. Justin Carr on the mound for the Rockets, in relief of Andy McClellan. Andy went a strong four innings, giving up only six hits and three walks. The two runs scored on back-to-back doubles in the second and one big mistake—a fastball up and in to Tim Brody—in the fourth.

Andy wanted the pitch back the moment he threw it, but of course it was too late. Brody swung those powerful arms and hit the ball a country mile. It went so far over the center field fence it bounced off a car on Hamilton Avenue.

Now it was up to Justin to finish the job. He gave up a lead-off single in the fifth, then retired the side on two ground balls and a strikeout. His low strikes were giving the Tornadoes fits, and coming into the sixth, he got the first two batters on another strikeout and a pop-up to Brian Krause at short. Then, suddenly, everything changed. Jeff Preston, the gritty Tornado third baseman, singled sharply to right, and Harry Gerardo, the center fielder, worked the count to 3 and 2 and walked!

Back behind the Raymondtown IGA, the crowd was getting restless. Head Coach Ron Channing, tall and dark, came out to the mound to talk with big, blond Justin. Luke Emory, the sparkplug catcher, came out, too. "Burn it in there, Jus'!" Phil Hubbard shouted from third.

Luke and Coach Channing left the mound. Justin pounded the ball into his glove. He seemed to have his confidence back. A good thing. The batter striding to the plate was Tim Brody.

Justin worked so slowly he drove the infielders crazy. He walked around on the mound. His windup was big and slow. But now, everyone was concentrating so hard it didn't matter. It was power against control, lefty against lefty. They had to get that final out!

Tim Brody stepped in and took a few practice swings. Everyone on the field took a deep breath and prayed.

Out in left field, Jenny Carr got into position. With two out, two on, and Brody at bat, she was playing deep. If the ball was hit hard on the fly, she could catch it for out number three. If there was a base hit past Phil or Brian, she could get in front of it and keep a run from scoring.

Jenny bent her knees and kept her hands in front of her. As Justin wound and fired a fastball for Strike 1, she got up on the balls of her feet.

Jenny was ready, but earlier on her mind had been wandering. Nothing had been hit to her since the third inning. She'd talked it up with Michael Wong in center and backed up every play by the infielders, but it was hard to go on doing that, never make a play of your own, and stay involved in the game.

Brody took Ball 1.

Nothing could distract her now. What she wanted most was for Brody to hit a fly ball right at her. She could reach up and squeeze it for the out, rush in, and get mobbed by her teammates. She could win it for the Rockets and win it for Justin. Justin was her twin brother, and she would do anything for him.

Brody fouled one off. Strike 2.

Of course it wasn't too likely that the ball would be hit to her. Lefties usually pulled the ball to right, and Brody's homer had been to right-center. But who could tell? Brody could cross everyone up, step into a pitch, and go to the opposite field. He could also swing late on a Justin fastball and hit one to left by accident.

A change-up way high and outside. Brody took Ball 2.

Jenny could feel the tension in the crowd. She could feel the taut nerves of the Rocket infielders, bent and ready in front of her. With the count 2 and 2, Brody wouldn't let too many go by.

Out of the corner of her eye, Jenny saw her father—Jack Carr, Coach Carr—in the Rockets' dugout. She saw him gesture with his hand, moving her a little further from the line toward center field.

She had just moved and got back into position when Justin wound and fired his next pitch. She knew it was the heater the moment it left his hand, and she knew it was trouble from the way Brody pounced.

The ball seemed to fly off his bat. It was high and deep and heading for left field! The crowd gasped. Would it make it to the fence? Would it go over?

Jenny watched the path of the ball. Her father had moved her into just the right position. She took a few steps back. What she'd imagined was about to happen. She was going to make this catch and win the game for Justin and the Rockets.

She held up her glove, her right hand bracing it on the side. But something happened with the wind. An unexpected gust—she would never know for sure—and suddenly the ball wasn't where she thought it would be. It was going too far, going over her head, going—!

She stepped back, reached up her glove, and hoped. The ball glanced off the webbing, caromed off the fence, and skittered toward the corner.

Jenny had fallen backwards on the play. She got up and ran for the ball. But the Tornado fans were cheering, and their runners were tearing around the bases. When she reached the ball, she panicked.

She knew she was supposed to throw to the cut-off man, Brian Krause. Two throws would get to the plate more

quickly than one. But Jenny saw a run-ner coming around third. She wasn't sure if he was the tying or the winning run, but she picked up the ball and threw as hard as she could toward home!

The throw was wild. It caromed off the backstop and bounced back toward the mound. By the time Justin was able to retrieve it and throw to Luke at the plate, two runs were in and Tim Brody was on third.

The Tornadoes were ahead 4–3, and Jenny thought she would die. She had let everyone down: her brother, her fa-ther, the team. Now the Rockets would lose, and it would be her fault. She wanted to crawl away somewhere and never be seen again.

But she couldn't. She was still playing left field, and there was still one out to get.

8

2. "You Stink!"

Jenny looked over at Michael Wong in center field. Apart from Justin, he was her best friend on the team.

Michael smiled and gave her the thumbs up sign. "Come on, Jen! It was a tough play. You did the best you could."

Jenny smiled back. She knew that wasn't really true. Missing the catch might have been excusable. Throwing the ball away was not. Even so, she felt a little better. She settled down and got ready for the next batter.

There wasn't much of a wait. Justin threw a fastball down and away, and an off-balance swing, a squibbed ground ball to Vicky Lopez at second, a crisp throw to Andy McClellan at first, and the Tornadoes were through.

But the damage was done. The Rockets came in to bat needing one to tie and two to win. If they came up empty, there was nowhere to go but home for dinner.

As Jenny trotted in from left, she almost wished Justin had taken longer to get the last batter out. The more time between her and her error, the less likely that it would seem so horrible. To her anyway. Maybe it would never seem less horrible to anyone else.

She passed her father at third base. She couldn't even look at him.

"Get back into it, Jen!" he called. "Everyone makes mistakes. Show 'em what you're made of."

"Thanks, Dad," she said, but she didn't really believe him. He was just saying those things because he was her father.

She hoped no one would talk to her. She reached the dugout and sat down at the very end of the bench. Michael Wong sat next to her, as if he were offering protection.

And the game went on. Trying too hard to blast one, Justin flied out to right. Then Brian walked, and big Pete Wyshansky came to the plate. Moving to the on-deck circle, Jenny took a few swings, put the doughnut on her bat and took a few more as she watched Pete work the count to 2 and 2, then lash a double to the gap in left-center.

Runners on second and third. One out. Now it was her turn. A base hit would tie the game, maybe even win it. A double would win it for sure. She could wipe away the hurt. All she had to do was get that hit!

It seemed like an awfully big task. All she could remember was the ball glancing off her glove, the panic as she forgot the cut-off man and threw as hard as she could toward home. She stepped into the batter's box and anchored her rear foot.

She got her arms back and tried to concentrate. She was so nervous, she could hardly see the pitcher, a big Hispanic kid named Manuel Rivera. He wound and threw, and she lunged at a lousy fastball, high and outside, for Strike 1.

"Stay in there, Jenny!" Michael shouted from the bench.

"Just meet the ball!" she heard her father.

She came all the way around on another fastball. Strike 2.

She was losing it, losing it all. She stepped out and tried to calm down. Coach Lopez came over and put his arm around her.

"Take it easy, Jen. Don't try to kill it. Listen to your father. Meet the ball."

She stepped back in, took a deep breath and let it go, swung the bat and got ready. The pitch was way outside and clearly wasted. The count moved to 1 and 2.

But Jenny was still deep in a hole. 1 and 2 left no room for error, and already Rivera was winding up. She wanted to say no, no, give me more time, but there was no more time. In came the pitch, right down the middle of the plate!

Jenny swung. She felt the click as her bat met the ball, felt terrific as she dropped the bat and took off for first base. She imagined the two runs scoring as she ran, imagined the cheers as the Rockets won the game after all.

There was a loud pop as her line drive smacked into the pocket of the short-stop's glove. He flipped to the second baseman, who touched the bag and doubled up Pete Wyshansky. Pete was two steps past second base. It all happened so fast, he couldn't even lean back toward the bag.

The game was over. The Tornadoes had won 4–3.

Jenny was so stunned, she hardly realized she was out. Then, gradually, it sank in. Not only had she not redeemed herself, she had ruined the rally and finalized the Rockets' defeat.

As she made her way back to the dugout, head down, sick at heart, Pete Wyshansky ran past her.

"You stink!" he bawled. "You only get to play 'cause your dad's a coach."

Jenny's mouth dropped open. She turned to say something in protest, but Pete was already in the dugout. Then she thought a moment. She had made an inexcusable error in the field. She had lined into a game-ending double play. But she was the Rockets' starting left fielder. That meant Coach Channing had confidence in her. It had to mean that, didn't it? He wouldn't do anything that wasn't for the good of the team. He wouldn't let her play just because of her father. Would he?

Her spirits sank so low she could hardly stand. She felt dizzy and weak. She couldn't go back into the dugout

14

where her teammates were packing up their gear and getting ready to go. Someone else might say something. She didn't make errors all the time. Didn't they realize that?

She sat down on first base and clasped her hands between her knees. Was she really such a lousy ballplayer? Jenny, whose brother was a star. Jenny, the coach's daughter.

Tears welled up, but she held them back. Someone was tugging at her shoulder.

She looked up. It was Michael.

"Jen," he said, "would you please forget this game? You had an off day, but it's over. Next game we'll win, and you'll be the hero."

Did he mean that? Was he just saying it because he liked her?

"Oh, Michael," she said, and burst out crying.

He sat beside her on the base and let her cry. When she had stopped crying, he heard his father call.

"I have to go, Jen. See you at school Monday."

Jenny nodded. "Thanks, Michael."

And then, there was her father. He came out of the dugout, heading for third base. It was always his job to collect the bases after a home game, but when he saw her on first, he walked over.

She watched him come. He was big and broad, with sandy-colored hair, a brush mustache, and large hands.

"Hi," he said.

"Hi," she said.

"Are you planning on taking that base home with you?"

"Only if I can use it as a pillow."

"Your mother might not like the idea."

"I know."

There was a pause, and Jack Carr said, "Are you okay?"

Jenny smiled. Could he have any idea what she was really thinking? If he did, would he ever tell her?

He pulled her up to him and hugged her. "Jen," he said, "you had a bad day. You can't let a couple of lousy breaks destroy your fun."

"Yeah," she said, "I'll do better next time."

Her dad hugged her again. "That's the spirit. Now let's go home. Will you help me with the bases?"

"Sure," said Jenny, but as they went from one to the next, she wondered: Is he just trying to be my dad instead of the coach?

3. Going Home

When Jenny and her father reached
the station wagon, Justin was already
in the front seat. Jenny got in the back.
Dad slipped in behind the wheel.

Justin looked out through the wind-
shield. He paid no attention to anyone.

And then Jenny remembered. Not only
had she lost the game for the Rockets.
She had lost the game for *Justin*!

When Justin relieved Andy McClellan
with the Rockets ahead 3–2, and the
Tornadoes came back and tied the
score and then went ahead, the game
became Justin's to win or lose. Now
that loss would go on his pitching re-
cord. Short of finding out her father
was playing her when she wasn't any

good, she couldn't imagine anything worse.

No wonder Justin didn't want to talk to her. He'd probably never talk to her again!

Coach Carr drove home through quiet streets. Jenny looked out at the shops on Market Street and at the grand homes along Symington Boulevard. When the coach had to stop for a light, he decided to break the silence.

"Tough loss today, Justin."

"Yeah, tough."

"Do you want to talk about it?"

"No."

"You don't think it might help?"

"No. Dad, could we just leave this alone?"

"Of course, but I'd like to say one thing."

"Sure."

"Things don't always go the way we want them to go. Sometimes they do, and sometimes they slip away. And when they slip away, it isn't necessarily anyone's fault. Everyone on a team is trying very hard to win, but when you don't, when something unexpected happens, you have to regroup and try even harder tomorrow."

Justin said nothing, but Jenny was dying in the back seat. Her father was trying to get Justin to forgive her. Or was he really trying to smooth things over so he could go on playing her no matter how bad she got? She didn't know, and she couldn't ask. All she could do was go on dying in the back seat.

The station wagon pulled into their driveway on Broadview Avenue. It was a long driveway with grass and trees. The house had a porch in front, and as the car pulled up, Mom came out and waited at the top of the steps.

Coach Carr opened the driver's side door. Then he turned to his son. "Justin, I know you've been disappointed today, but you have to remember we're out there to have fun. If we're not having fun, there's no point."

"I understand, Dad," said Justin. "Just give me a little time."

"Okay. Let's go say hi to your mother."

Jenny didn't want to say hi to her mother. She wanted to spend the night in the back seat of the station wagon, hiding in the dark garage. But she opened the door on her side, climbed out, and followed her father and brother up the stairs.

"Hello, big leaguers," said Mom, and hugged them all. "Did you have a terrific afternoon?"

"Maybe we should talk at dinner," Dad said.

Mom and Dad exchanged a look. "Okay," said Mom, "everyone to the showers. Dinner's in half an hour."

Jenny went to her room. She stood in the middle and looked around. There was her Rah Rah Rockets pennant. There was her trophy for most improvement in T-ball. Against the bureau was an extra bat and the first glove she had ever had and no longer used. There was a doll and a teddy bear, too, but everything about this room said ballplayer.

She walked over to her mirror. Her dark blond pony tail was coming undone. There was a smudge on her face and one on her neck. The uniform she loved was dirty and had a small tear in the sleeve. She was a skinny girl with a nose she thought was too long, but everything about her said ballplayer!

When Jenny reached the dinner table, Dad and Justin were already there. She took her seat, and Mom served the meat loaf, mashed potatoes, and green beans. She had taken only a few bites when Mom said, "Dad tells me things didn't go so well today. I'm just glad that both of you are bigger than any baseball game."

There was a long, painful silence.

Jenny took another forkful of meat loaf, but she couldn't make herself put it in her mouth.

"She lost the game for me, Mom," Justin said.

"Justin!" said Dad. "That isn't true, and you know it! Apologize to Jenny at once!"

But Justin couldn't stop himself. "It is true, Dad. Anybody could have caught Brody's fly ball. It was just so . . . so *dumb* . . . to miss it, and that throw . . ."

"That's enough, Justin! Is *this* what you call needing a little more time? Is this what you call sportsmanship?"

Jenny didn't know what to call any of it, and she didn't care. All she knew was that Justin was right, and it hurt. She put down her fork and burst into tears. Then she ran from the table and slammed the door to her room.

25

4. "Who Is It?"

For a long time she sobbed into her pillow. She could hear raised voices in the dining room, but she paid no attention. Why did Justin have to say those things, even if he knew they were true? She wasn't a cleanup hitter and a pitcher like him, but he'd always said she was good enough to start. Was he only just saying that *because their father had made him say it*?

She wished she could wipe this whole game away, just take it back to the beginning and start over again. Then everything could come out differently, and none of these awful words would ever have been spoken.

A while later, there was a knock on her door. "Jenny?" said her mom.

"Yes."

"I've left your dinner on the kitchen table."

"Thanks."

There was quiet. It was getting dark. Jenny wasn't hungry, and she wasn't sleepy. She just lay there on the bed surrounded by misery.

There was another knock on the door.

"Who is it?" Jenny asked.

"It's me, Justin."

"What do you want? Haven't you said enough already?"

"I want to talk to you."

"Oh, all right. Come in."

Jenny jumped off the bed, turned on the light, and unlocked the door. Justin trooped in, looking sheepish.

"Can I sit down?" he asked.

"Sure. Sit."

Justin sat in Jenny's desk chair. Jenny sat on the bed. She folded her arms.

"So?"

Justin looked at her. She was always better with words than he. How could he say what he had to say?

"I'm sorry I said what I did at the table," he began.

"Is this you or is this Mom and Dad?"

"It's me. I was very upset you lost me the game."

"I know you were upset. I was more upset than you. But couldn't we have talked about it the way we always talk about things? Did you have to stick it out there in front of Mom and Dad?"

"No. That's why I'm apologizing."

"And after all that stuff Dad said in the car about having fun and trying harder tomorrow."

"I wasn't listening very well. Jenny, I'm apologizing."

"I accept your apology, and I'm sorry about the game. But we're still ballplayers, aren't we, Justin? Still, the two of us, ballplayers?"

"Sure. One day—a couple of mistakes—doesn't change anything."

"Shake on it."

They shook.

"Great. Now I'm hungry. I think I'll go eat my dinner."

"When you're finished, want to watch TV with me?"

"I'll bring my food along."

Jenny found her plate in the kitchen. The food was cold, but she didn't care. She brought it into the living room and ate as she and Justin watched a sitcom about funny old ladies. Then they watched a movie about some fancy people doing mean things to each other a long time ago.

Jenny was pleased to be with Justin and so pleased he had apologized. But all the while she sat with him, she wondered: Would he *really* want me playing if Dad wasn't the coach and he could have anyone he wanted? Wouldn't he rather see Ken Bernstein or Adam Spinelli starting in left field?

5. Dolls and Dreams

The next day, Sunday, Jenny had breakfast with her family. Everyone seemed low-key and friendly. All the awful feelings had gone away.

As Dad read the Sunday paper and Mom poured a second cup of coffee, Jenny wondered what they would do today. The Rockets' usual Sunday game was canceled. It would be played Wednesday afternoon instead. Would they do some practicing? Would they go for a drive?

"Jenny," Mom said between sips, "I hope you haven't forgotten your date with Heather this afternoon."

Oh, no. Of course she'd forgotten. Heather was a girl at school who wanted

31

to be friends. She was nice but too whiny. She wasn't good at sports either.

"Oh, Mom," Jenny said, "do I have to?"

"Of course you have to. You made this date more than a week ago. Heather would be hurt if you didn't come."

"She made me make it. Mom, I don't want to."

"Jenny . . ."

"Oh, all right."

The rest of the morning, she flopped around the house. She did some reading, oiled the pocket of her glove, had a catch with Justin on the back lawn. At lunch she decided she would wear jeans and sneakers. Promptly at one-thirty, she was ready.

Mom drove her over to Heather's. As they pulled into the driveway, Mrs. Jenkins came out.

"How nice to see you, Jenny. Heather is so excited about your coming."

"That's nice," said Jenny.

"I'll be back around four-thirty," said Mom.

"How's four?" said Jenny.

"Jen—"

"Okay, okay."

She followed Mrs. Jenkins into the house. At the foot of the stairs, all lined up, were a million different dolls. Well, maybe not a million, but at least twenty.

"Hi!" yelled Heather, leaping out from behind a door. "We *all* wanted to say hi."

Jenny was mystified. "Hi," she said, "to all of you."

"Will you help carry them up?" Heather whispered. "Then we can play."

Jenny and Heather carried all the dolls back to Heather's room. When they'd finished giving them tea from the special miniature china tea set, Heather asked, "Do you like ballet? I just love to dance."

"I like baseball," Jenny said.

"I like watching it on TV," said

Heather. "I wish I were a better player. Would you like to see me dance?"

"Sure," said Jenny. "I don't mind dancing."

Heather got up and danced around the room. In her pink dress, she looked lovely against the pink and white flowers on the wallpaper, and the pink and white flowers on the bedspread and chair.

She did many steps and several leaps and twirls.

"You're good," Jenny said.

"Thank you," said Heather. "I take classes. You could take some, too."

"I like being outside," said Jenny. "I like hitting the ball and having teammates."

Clearly Heather was disappointed. She stopped dancing and sat back down on the floor. "Sometimes I dream about dancing in a great big theater," she said. "I finish, and everyone applauds."

"I dream about hitting a home run and winning the game for the Rockets," Jenny said.

"Do you think you'll ever do it?"

"I don't know, but I'll keep trying."

"I'm the same way about my dancing," Heather said, but Jenny hardly heard her. She'd realized that what she'd said was true. She really loved baseball and loved getting better at it. She didn't know how many people felt she was only playing because her dad was a coach, but she'd go on trying to prove herself every day.

"Would you like a snack?" Heather asked.

"Oh," Jenny said, "sure. I'd love one," but what she really wanted to say was how grateful she was to Heather for giving her back her courage.

The feeling lasted until Monday—the very next day—at school.

Jenny arrived with Justin. She was brimming with confidence. Saturday was far away. A new week was beginning. She sat in her seat in Mrs. Irvington's class. Then she had to go to the bathroom.

36

She raised her hand. Mrs. Irvington gave her permission, but on the way back, she ran into Pete Wyshansky and Andy McClellan at the water fountain.

Pete finished drinking and looked up. "Hey," he said, "look who's here. It's Coach Carr's little darling."

"Yeah," said Andy, "the no-field, no-hit kid."

"You wonder why they let her play. Of course we could always ask her daddy . . ."

"She's not even good for a girl."

"They probably play her *because* she's a girl—"

"Stop it, stop it!" Jenny yelled.

Her eyes filled with tears. She stumbled away and groped for Mrs. Irvington's door. When she found it, she pulled herself together, then tried to sneak in so no one would notice.

But Mrs. Irvington did. "Jenny, are you okay?" she asked.

"I'm fine," Jenny said. She tried not to look at Mrs. Irvington.

Her world had come apart again. Pete would never leave her alone, and now there was Andy McClellan. Andy, the hard-throwing pitcher, whom she'd always sort of liked. How many others would join them? How many more felt the way they did and would never say? Was she really only playing because of her father? The question came back and stabbed at her again.

6. Which Way to Turn

She wanted to talk to Justin. He was sitting right across the aisle, but language arts class was beginning and she couldn't say a thing. Pete and Andy slouched in and sat down up front. Neither one of them looked at her.

How was she going to get through the morning? She didn't know, but somehow language arts passed and so did math. Mrs. Irvington must have known something was wrong. She didn't call on her at all, but as the class was getting ready for gym, she said, "Jenny, stay a minute."

Jenny got nervous. She couldn't talk to her teacher about what had happened or what she felt.

"Yes, Mrs. Irvington."

"Is something the matter? You seemed miles away this morning."

"I wasn't feeling so well. Now I'm okay."

"Will you please tell me if you don't feel well again?"

"Yes."

"All right. Off you go."

Jenny ran to gym. All they were doing today was calisthenics, and she did them without thinking. She hoped she could talk to Justin at lunch, but when she got to the cafetorium, he was already there and busy with Luke and Brian. She sat by herself, and Michael Wong sat beside her.

"Hi, Jen."

"Hi, Michael."

"Ready for practice tomorrow?"

"Sure. Can't wait."

She couldn't tell Michael anything either. He was part of the team. He might get the wrong idea.

They talked about the upcoming game

against the Badgers. Then they went back to class.

For a moment, passing Vicky Lopez in the hall, Jenny thought she might talk to her after school. Since Vicky's father was a coach too, she might understand. But Vicky was such a solid player she probably never had doubts like Jenny's. She'd probably think Jenny was crazy.

By the time the day was over, Jenny just wanted to go home. Justin had a piano lesson across town, so she took the school bus by herself.

Her dad was a lawyer; her mom was a travel agent in town. Usually no one was home until after five, but as Jenny climbed the front steps, she heard someone inside.

She climbed the rest of the way on tiptoe. Carefully she opened the door. A figure was standing in the hall. She jumped back, then realized it was her mother.

"Oh, Mom!" she said, and ran into her arms.

"Jenny, Jenny, what is it?" Mom said, and the whole story came pouring out.

When Jenny was through, Mom said, "Well, I'm certainly glad I came home early today. Why don't we have some tea and talk about this?"

They went into the kitchen, and when the kettle was on, Jenny finally asked her question. "Mom," she said, "could Dad be letting me play just because I'm his daughter?"

Mom took the kettle off the stove and poured the tea. They sat at the kitchen table, the red and white checked cloth between them.

"I don't think so," Mom said. "Your father isn't that kind of man. But why don't you talk to him about this your-self? He'd want to know you're upset."

Jenny thought about how hard it would be to confront her father. Again, she heard him telling the story he wanted her to hear.

"I can't do that," she said. "Please don't tell him I told you anything."

Mom squeezed Jenny's hand. "I won't, but try not to worry about this too much. Those kids are just being mean because they lost the game. You know how good you are."

I know, thought Jenny, and she remembered how confident she'd been at Heather's. A million years ago, before the water fountain disaster. But now her mother had helped bring back her spirits. When she arrived at practice the next day, she was ready to work.

Her father couldn't leave the office, but Coach Lopez was there, hitting fly balls to the outfielders. Jenny went to join them as Justin headed for the bullpen to start warming up his pitching arm.

It was a beautiful spring day. The outfield grass smelled sweet and fresh, and as she hauled in her first long fly and powered her throw to the cut-off man, Jenny felt a surge of pride.

"Good catch!" she heard from across the outfield.

It was Michael Wong. She gave him the thumbs-up sign, and he gave it back.

Another fly and she was under it, remembering to make the catch over her throwing shoulder, step back with her throwing side, right foot, and keep the throw low and accurate.

She punched her fist into her glove, bent her knees, got ready again. So ready, she hardly even noticed Pete Wyshansky ignoring her on the other side of Michael.

Then it was time to field grounders. Down on one knee for the easy ones or play them like an infielder. Get down and look that ball into your glove. Plant your throwing-side foot, step toward the target, and throw. With runners on base, charge the ball, stride toward the target, make sure that throw is sharp. Keep it going! Feeling good!

After a while, Coach Lopez said, "Okay, everybody in to home plate. Coach Channing wants to talk to you."

The talk was about sliding. They hadn't been practicing it enough, and the coach went over the fundamentals. Begin your slide about ten feet from the base. If you're right-handed, start by striding with your left foot, then tuck it under your right thigh. The other way around for a lefty. Slide on your bottom and your lower back. Aim for the middle of the base. Keep your legs relaxed and your hands off the ground.

"Okay," said Coach Channing, "everyone line up at first base. We're all going to slide into second."

The coach demonstrated in a cloud of dust, then asked if there were any questions. There weren't, so they began.

Brian Krause went first, slid gracefully in, and popped up on his feet. Andy McClellan looked a little awkward, and Jenny had to keep herself from laughing when Pete Wyshansky tripped and practically fell on his face.

As for her, she loved it. Each time

45

around, she got the rhythm right, tucked her left leg under, kept her hands off the ground. When the coach finally said "Very good. That's enough. Time for hitting practice," she didn't want to stop.

But if she had to stop, the next best thing was hitting. She watched Luke Emory tee off on a few, then urged Michael on as he kept bouncing grounders to short. When it was her turn, she noticed Andy McClellan make a face and say something to Pete.

All right, you guys, Jenny said to herself. She stepped into the batter's box, faced Coach Lopez, and slammed the first pitch deep to left.

Then she stepped out, put her hand on her hip, and looked right at Pete and Andy. So there. Actions speak louder than words.

7. Getting a Chance

Wednesday. 3:30. Game time. Ready for the Badgers, who weren't supposed to be so great. Little Josh Rubin, the sidearm magician, was starting for the Rockets. Someone named Sonny Trout, whom no one had ever heard of, was pitching for the Badgers.

"Who is this guy?" Justin asked as he and Jenny got the news.

"Sounds pretty fishy to me," said Luke.

"Let's hope he's not too slippery," said Phil.

Everyone laughed, and Coach Channing called them all out for calisthenics. When they were warmed up and had completed a brisk pre-game practice, the coach posted the lineup for the game.

Jenny hurried over to see. With Josh pitching, Andy McClellan was in center field in place of Michael Wong. The other players were in their usual positions. Justin was starting at first of course, and there she was: *Jennifer Carr, LF*, batting seventh behind *Pete Wyshansky, RF*. Whatever the reasons, nothing had changed.

Mid-week game. Small crowd, but as the national anthem ended, Jenny was pleased to see her father race into the dugout half in and half out of his suit. Was he the one keeping her in the lineup? She didn't care. It was great he could get away for the game!

She hugged him, then picked up her glove and started for the outfield. She stopped when she passed Michael Wong, sitting on the bench.

"Sorry you're not starting, Michael."

"It's okay, as long as we win."

Jenny wished she had that kind of spirit. She wanted the team to win, but she wanted to be out there playing just as much.

Josh was wild from the beginning. He walked the first two Badgers he faced, then struck out one and gave up a towering double to the cleanup hitter, Lou Cohen. Two runs came home, and by the time Josh got the third out—a line drive Jenny caught right at the letters—the Badgers were ahead 4–0.

Jenny was glad to make the catch, glad to get the Rockets out of the inning, glad to feel she'd already done something positive in the game, even if it wasn't very fancy. But 4–0 in the bottom of the first wasn't very terrific, and what would this kid Sonny Trout turn out to be like?

He was little and fat. He had red hair and glasses. He had a tight, jerky windup and a high kick, and when the Rockets saw him warming up, they thought he was a joke.

"You think this guy can get the ball

over the plate?" Pete Wyshansky wondered out loud.

"Who knows if he'll even *reach* the plate?" said Andy McClellan.

Unfortunately for the Rockets, Sonny Trout could do both. He got Luke Emory on a weak tap back to the mound and Phil Hubbard on a pop-up to second base. Then, with three straight searing fastballs, he struck out Andy McClellan.

Wow! thought Jenny as she headed back to left. This game ain't no piece of cake.

Fortunately for the Rockets, Josh settled down in the top of the second. He struck out the first Badger hitter, threw a scare into everyone by walking the next, then got two ground balls to Vicky Lopez to retire the side.

Bottom of the second. Still 4–0. Already the crowd was getting restless.

"Rah Rah Rockets!" came a shout, but it was just one person.

The Rockets could do nothing against

52

this kid Trout. Justin walked on a 3–2 count to start the inning, then stole second with a picture-book slide on a close play. Everyone on the bench came alive, but it was no use. Brian and Pete Wyshansky both struck out, and Jenny cracked a deep fly to center that was caught three steps from the fence.

Not wonderful, Jenny thought as she trotted back to left. But at least I got it out of the infield! She looked right at Andy McClellan, but he didn't look back. That's better than anyone else so far! she wanted to shout.

It was better than anyone else would do for the next two innings. Josh held the Badgers to two walks and a bloop single, but Sonny Trout didn't let another ball out of the infield. He struck out two and walked two, but the rest were a smattering of ground balls and pop-ups. Luke Emory reached first on a bad-hop grounder the shortstop couldn't handle, and Phil bunted him along and managed to be safe at first, but that was about as much excitement as the Rockets could produce.

Then, in the top of the fifth, Josh began to tire. He struck out the first batter, went 0 and 2 on the first baseman, Tom Rollins, came unstrung, and lost him. As Rollins ran down to first, Josh paced on the mound. Just how far things had gone became clear when he went 3 and 0 on Lou Cohen, got desperate, and served up a meaty fastball on the outside corner.

Cohen belted a triple to right, the run scored, and the Badgers led 5–0.

That was all for Josh, but it was all for the Badgers, too. Brian Krause came in in relief and neatly put out the side. He didn't have great stuff, but he was accurate. One batter went down swinging, another flied out to Andy, and then, in the best play of the afternoon, Brian picked Lou Cohen off third base. Cohen had taken too big a lead, wasn't paying attention, and that was that.

Now it was the bottom of the fifth. 5–0 Badgers with time beginning to run short. Vicky Lopez struck out, but Luke blooped a single into short left field and Phil, waiting for his pitch, waiting until 3 and 2, doubled him over to third.

Second and third with one gone. Sonny Trout was proving human after all, but when he walked Andy McClellan on four pitches, that was the end of it. The skinny Badger manager headed for the mound, and Sonny headed for the bench.

"That's a shame," said Brian. "I wanted another shot at that guy."

"Me, too," said Jenny, who had popped to third her last time up.

"Yeah, I bet," Pete whispered under his breath.

Jenny said nothing, but she could feel the anger rising. You wait, wise guy, she said to herself. You'll get yours.

Now there was a relief pitcher warming up. He was a scrawny kid, but his fastball looked as if it had some pop.

When he was introduced as Henry Bartholomew, the Rocket bench tried hard not to giggle.

How could they? They might have the bases loaded, but they were still behind 5–0!

Bartholomew not only had a fastball and a change-up. He had something that looked close to a curve, a pitch that seemed to flutter and break over the corners. He threw two of those near-curves past Justin, but the next pitch was a fastball up and away, a pitch so ripe you could taste it.

Justin teed off, and the ball leaped into center field. The second baseman jumped high, but he had no chance. The center fielder charged the ball and fielded it neatly on the big hop, but when the dust had cleared, two runs were in, Andy McClellan was on third, and Justin was at first, cheering.

Then it was Brian's turn. He fouled off one of those near-curves, took two balls, dug in, and waited. Bartholomew ground the ball into his glove, wound and threw. A change-up down and in and Brian put it into right. Andy scored from third, but Justin had to hold at second.

It was now 5–3, runners on first and second, and still only one out, with Pete Wyshansky coming to the plate. He took Strike 1. He took Strike 2. He hauled off and swung at a near-curve, and he was out of there.

The Rockets were stunned. As Jenny passed Pete on her way to the plate, he avoided her.

Jenny smiled. *Big* Pete Wyshansky! And now here she was, two out and two on, the Rockets behind by two. It was her chance.

8. Crash Landing

Jenny settled into the batter's box, watched Henry Bartholomew, watched his motion, kept her eye on the ball.

He threw her a near-curve for Ball 1. He threw her a fastball, and she missed it.

"Come on, Jenny!" she heard from the bench. "Do it!"

She watched the *B* on Bartholomew's cap, watched the ball come over the top. It was a fastball, and she met it perfectly.

The ball sprang off her bat. It was a hard shot to left, just how hard she couldn't quite tell but easily for extra bases if it wasn't caught. She took off for first, watched the flight of the ball, heard the cheers of the crowd as the left fielder misplayed the carom and the ball landed in the corner.

She rounded first and headed for second, rounded second and headed for third! She'd driven in two runs. The score was now 5–5. She had to make it to third. They'd be so close to winning!

Her father was in the third base coaching box. He was crouching with his hands held out. Stop! he was telling her, but she couldn't stop. She had to get to third, had to prove how good she was, had to show them all!

Where was the ball? She couldn't see the ball. She forgot everything she'd learned about sliding and dove for the base.

There was a jolting feeling in her arms. Grit filled her mouth and eyes, and the wind popped out of her. There was a stunned silence and then voices. Someone—she thought it was her father—helped her off the field to the dugout. When she started breathing easily

again, her mother drove her home. She slept for awhile, and when she woke up, Justin was sitting across the room.

"Hi," she said, glad he was there.

"How are you feeling?"

"A little woozy. Was I safe?"

"No."

"Did we win?"

"No. We lost 6–5 in the sixth."

"I shouldn't have tried for third."

"Are you sure you want to talk about this now? I mean, you had a very hard knock, Jen."

"Yes. Now."

"All right. With two out and the score tied, you never try for the extra base at third. Second's just as good because you'll score from second on almost any base hit. Dad even said he told you to stop, but you missed the sign or something."

Jenny looked up. Her parents had slipped into the room while Justin was talking.

"Justin's right," said Dad, "but let's

not worry about that. What's important is you're okay."

Jenny thought she might explode. She'd told her father nothing of what she'd felt, nothing of what she'd been going through. Now she'd made everything worse.

"I missed your sign on purpose," she said.

"Jen," said Dad, "I—"

"It's true. I didn't care about the sign. I had to get to third because I had to prove how good I was."

"You know that isn't how we play the game."

"I had to prove how good I was, Dad, because these kids were saying I only got to play because you're my father."

There. It was said. Finally.

Dad looked shocked. "That's not so, Jen. Coach Channing wouldn't allow anything like that. You play because you're a topnotch outfielder."

"I knew you'd say that. Can I believe you?"

"I sure hope so. It's the truth."

"You're not just saying it because Justin is a star and you know how much I want to play too?"

"Certainly not. If I didn't think you were good enough, I would tell you. Why would I want you out there embarrassing yourself? If you liked playing, I wouldn't stop you from trying out, but I wouldn't let you start. I do have an obligation to the team, you know."

Jenny lay there for a moment, taking it all in.

"I told you I thought you were a ballplayer," Justin said. "You make mistakes, but everyone does. I wouldn't lie to you."

That did it. Jenny smiled. Her father *and* her brother believed in her. They knew she was good. Who cared what other people said?

She sat up. Her room was getting dark. Everyone was turning into shadows. She switched on her bedside lamp and remembered how helpful her mother had been. "Thanks, guys," she said. "I'm glad you're my family."

Her parents hugged her. Justin sort of hugged her, too.

"You get some rest, Jen," Mom said.

"Your mother's right," said Dad, "but about that headfirst slide—"

"Jack!" said Mom, "you're terrible."

She hustled him out the door. Justin followed, waving.

Jenny was alone. She would not slide headfirst again. She switched off the lamp and lay in the growing dark, dreaming of the Raymondtown ballpark and the crowd roaring approval as she drove in the winning run.

9. Not a Shadow of a Doubt

The next day Jenny was pretty stiff and sore.

"We know you're okay," said Mom, "but maybe you should stay home from school today. I'll take the day off to be with you."

That was nice. They played games and read, and there was time to rest and talk. But Jenny was ready to get going Friday. There were things she was missing at school. There was baseball practice.

As if it were any other day, Dad dropped her off with Justin on his way to work. The two of them wandered in, wearing their backpacks, carrying their baseball gloves.

From nowhere, Michael Wong appeared. "Were you hurt, Jen? Can you play?"

Jenny laughed. "Don't be so upset, Michael. I'm fine."

Then Vicky Lopez asked if she was all right, and Luke and Phil and Brian asked, too. Classes flew by, and it wasn't until lunch that Pete Wyshansky made a face at her. She made a better face back, so it didn't even matter.

School let out. She and Justin got dressed at their lockers, then hurried to the ballfield.

As they arrived, Jenny saw Coach Channing gesture to her from the dugout. Uh oh, she thought, what now? Justin wished her luck and headed for first base.

The coach motioned for Jenny to sit beside him. When she did, a little nervously, he said, "I hope you're in good shape. No bones broken. No spirits broken either."

Jenny shrugged. "Everything's fine, Coach."

"I'm glad. We've got a tough game tomorrow."

There was a pause. The coach folded his arms and stroked his beard.

"May I assume," he said, "that your father has had some words with you about missing his sign and sliding head-first?"

Jenny tried not to giggle. "Yes," she said.

"Good. Now get out there and show me some hustle!"

Whew! thought Jenny, dashing to the outfield. She hustled through the drill with Coach Lopez, got a few solid hits with Coach Channing pitching, even saw him smiling as she slammed a change-up into center field.

But then practice was over, and the coach was waving everyone to the mound for an announcement. "The Bulldogs' field in Bradford isn't playable," he began. "Tomorrow's game will be at home instead. This should work out fine because you may remember everyone's due here at nine for our team photograph. Please brush your hair and show up in clean uniforms."

Jenny was so excited, she could hardly eat dinner. Then it was hard to get to sleep. When she finally did, it seemed like morning a moment later.

She got dressed in the uniform she loved. Now she'd get to have her picture taken in it!

Breakfast was an afterthought. She and Justin and their father arrived at the ballfield before anyone else.

The other Rockets straggled in around 9:15. By then a funny little man with frizzy gray hair was setting up his camera at the mound. The players formed three rows, shortest to tallest, with the coaches on either side. Justin was in the back. Jenny got to be in the middle between Michael and Adam Spinelli. She had a great big smile when the shutter clicked.

68

When the picture-taking was over, the players hung around for awhile. Jenny was talking with Michael and Luke when she noticed Pete say something to Andy and point in her direction. She knew what that had to be about and shrugged it off, but Coach Channing was passing by and overheard.

"What's that, Pete?" he asked.

"Oh, nothing, Coach."

"Come over here a minute."

Suddenly they were arguing. Then Pete stalked off, shouting and gesturing. Jenny didn't know what had been said, but it felt like a victory for the good guys.

She and Justin went home for lunch. They got back to the ballpark at one-thirty. It was time for stretches and wind-sprints, time to get going.

When Coach Channing posted the lineup, Jenny held her breath. There was her name, starting in left, but she was batting sixth, not seventh! Ken

Bernstein was starting in right and batting in Jenny's usual seventh spot.

Who could believe it? Pete Wyshansky had been benched!

The game started out like a shot. Justin was pitching, and he gave up two singles and a homer in the top of the first. But the Rockets came right back. A big, strong righthander named Rick Martino was pitching for the Bulldogs. He was fast, but he seemed to have no control.

With his very first pitch, he hit Luke Emory. Fortunately Luke wasn't hurt. He danced down to first, and Phil Hubbard promptly singled him over to third. Andy McClellan skyed to right, but it was deep enough for Luke to tag up and score on the sacrifice.

Phil had to hold at first, but Justin was coming to the plate. In his usual methodical way, he waited Martino out, and Martino was wild enough so he could do it. At 2 and 0, a wild pitch moved Phil over to second, but it turned out not to matter. Justin took a couple of strikes, but with the count 3 and 2, he got his pitch, a fastball on the outside corner, and cranked it into the right field bleachers.

The crowd went wild. Brian Krause bounced to short and Jenny popped to second, but at the end of the first inning, the score was tied 3–3.

It stayed that way for awhile. Jenny wasn't so pleased about her pop-up, but she made two good catches in left in the third, and kept a runner at second with a solid throw to Brian in the fourth.

By the bottom of the fourth, it was still 3–3.

Jenny led off for the Rockets. She took two balls and a strike, then lashed a fastball down the third base line, came around first, kept on going, and made a perfect slide into second. As she stood up, called time, and dusted herself off, she saw Pete Wyshansky scowling at the end of the bench.

Let him scowl! Maybe the bench would teach him a lesson.

But the rally went nowhere. At the top of the sixth, the score was Bulldogs 3, Rockets 3.

Justin got the first two outs in the inning, but things unraveled after that. He gave up a walk and back-to-back singles, and the Bulldogs squeezed in a run. Andy replaced Justin and put out the fire, but the Rockets came up for their last licks trailing 4–3.

Rick Martino was still out there, but Justin got to him early. He put his first fastball into center field and cruised into second with a stand-up double. Then Brian Krause settled in and walked.

Jenny coming up. Two men on and nobody out. The game on the line but room to breathe. She took the first pitch. Ball 1. She took the second pitch. Ball 2. She looked down the third base line at her father. He touched the peak of his cap. At 2 and 0, the sign was hit away!

The next pitch was coming, a good fat fastball. Jenny watched it, and then she swung. The ball took off, deep into the gap in left-center, and she began to run.

As she rounded first, she saw Justin coming in to score. As she rounded second, Brian reached the plate. She held at second for a moment, the way she was supposed to, but it didn't matter. The cheers swept over her. A full-fledged Rocket, a starting Rocket, she had driven in the winning run.